The Corn
(Stories and

By Benjan

Cover: *'Beata Beatrix'*
By Dante Gabriel Rossetti.

Copyright © 2020 Benjamin James Elliott

ISBN: 9798558797589

All rights reserved, including the right to reproduce this book, or portions thereof in any form. No part of this text may be reproduced, transmitted, downloaded, decompiled, reverse engineered, or stored, in any form or introduced into any information storage and retrieval system, in any form or by any means, whether electronic or mechanical without the express written permission of the author.

__Introduction.__

Darkness and light, two sides of the spectrum, and the two sides of the same coin. These are familiar to us, but what of that gap in between the light and the dark? What about that 'grey' area where things are neither shrouded in darkness or illuminated by the light? This is what I have sought to bring you in the first of my collection of short stories.

Each story represents a state of being, and a state of mind. These 'states' are very much part of the foggy area between corporeal and cerebral existence, and draw on the strands of fiber that connect these two things together.

I'm sure that you are able to draw on your own experiences in life that have left you in a state of unease or confusion, and that this has in some measure brought about questions on the nature of your own sense of 'reality'. This is perfectly normal, and our brains are very well adept at pushing these feelings and thoughts to the back of our minds, and out of the way.

But, consider for a moment what it would be like if you were forced to face certain realities, or if you were unable push aside what is happening to you in the present moment. This is where I want you to be. Neither in the dark, or fully illuminated. Neither in a dream, or in a nightmare.

The ultimate meaning of each story I leave up to you, as I do not wish to go any further into the explanations behind each narrative. This is because, as I have stated in my other works, the perception of the reader is paramount in helping forge the wider scope of understanding that all literary works need when they are released by the author into the wider world.

B. Elliott

God-Notes: (**Noun**) *also known as 'divine notes' or 'celestial resonance'*

A series of musical notes, that in the correct combination evoke within the listener a feeling of divine or other worldly emotions and sensations.

The notes, or combination of notes, must be played at a particular pace and frequency. This can be achieved by the use of certain instruments. String, or brass for example.

Considering that all forms of life are made up of atoms, and these atoms are vibrating constantly, it is thought that these vibrations create a frequency. The frequency of life you might say. In turn, these vibrations and frequencies can be mimicked by the use of instruments in the making of music.

It is said that when a person dies, they experience a wave of 'frequency' wash over them. For those who have temporarily been declared clinically dead, this is something they have testified to having experienced once resuscitated. This experience is said to be completely unique, and emotionally elating.

It could be said, that music created at the exact pitch and frequency as this 'wave' could account for why humans are moved so profoundly by certain kinds of composition. Almost a musical nod to the afterlife, if you will.

1.
Alfa and Omega.

At 8:46 on a cold Autumn morning, Peter Watkins, aged 83, died. As the darkness encroached on his vision, and the last of his familiar surroundings melted away into a blur, he felt all sensations slip away. Even the fur on his tongue no longer registered. This was the end.

Nothing existed. Not even the small pain at the base of his back, or the age-old pain located behind his right knee. It was as if his entire body had evaporated, and all that remained was his brain, floating in mid-air. But how could this be? Peter was still conscious, he was still thinking, he could still imagine. So, how come he couldn't even feel his brain?

Peter dared to open his eyes. That was if he still had eye lids to open, or even eyes to see! Or was he now locked in an invisible cage? A cage of eternal darkness.

As the lids of his eyes opened, it was as if opening them for the very first time. A bright, brilliant light burst into his vision, so powerful it felt as though it was punching straight through him like a lightning bolt. In one side, and out the other. Peter began to panic. He looked all around himself, but could see nothing, just the pure brilliance of light.

Something felt wrong. He was panicking, but not in a way he was familiar with. This was a sort of calm panic, a panic of the mind, not of the body. He couldn't even feel the beat of his heart in his chest, or the hot tingling of anxiety in his brow. Nothing. Was this even panic?

He wanted to run his hands through his wispy white hair, as if to grasp at the reality of the situation, but try as he might he couldn't. He looked down, but there was nothing! He tried to bring his hands up to his face, but there was nothing.

As if from nowhere, something in Peters mind suddenly sparked into life. He didn't know what it was, or where it came from, but it had a heavy, significant feeling about it.

In that moment, to lend perspective on his surroundings, a figure appeared in front of him. Not in a physical form, but a mental form. Peter could see this figure in his mind, but the figure had no substance, no outline, no movement. It was just there!

Peter waited. He had no idea what was going on. Time seemed to drift and flow around him, almost as if it wasn't there. No fixed points. He just waited.

Ω

It felt like an eternity. Or, had it actually been an eternity? An eternity of waiting, not knowing, just watching the figure in front of him. Peter dared to ask a question.

"Where am I?" The words made no sound, they just happened. They were just said.

The figure responded. "You are in a world of humanities creation. A world born at the very moment the first human became aware of itself, and asked its very first question."

Peter knew this figure was telling the truth, but couldn't quite understand what it meant. "How is this possible?"

The figure looked at Peter, and smiled, without smiling. "My dear friend, the moment we first appeared on the earth and became aware of ourselves, we gave birth to true consciousness. This consciousness, having no physical form, could last beyond the bounds of the body, and transcend into true consciousness after death."

Peter thought. Could this be possible? Could he really have transcended his earthly existence, or was this just some crazy dream? No, it couldn't be, somehow he knew it couldn't be. It was as if his mind was now open, completely open!

The figure spoke again. "Comprehend, Peter. Let it happen, don't fight it. Now that your mind is open and free you must allow it to expand".

It was as if the entirety of the universe was in Peters' mind. Suddenly everything became limitless, and the illusion of time had played its final cord. The past, the present, and the future could be seen in a single moment.

"So, this isn't an afterlife, but more of a re-life?" Peter asked. The figure nodded, without nodding. "Yes, that's correct. You haven't died, and yet you are no longer alive. You haven't been reborn, because your existence continues." It made perfect sense. Peter, in that moment, could see it all so clearly. But what now?

The figure understood. "You have all the time now. You have the entire universe and beyond to explore. All it takes is your mind, because that is all you are now. Nothing more, nothing less".

The figure receded from Peter, and he was left alone to consider not just himself, but the limitless possibilities at his cerebral fingertips. Time passed, without passing. Suns had risen, and suns had set. Stars came and went, and events just became another horizon in the distance.

It was around this time, without time, that Peter met other figures. Each one the same, but simultaneously different. They spoke with him. Some spoke of the experiences they had had together with him, and others talked, without talking, of their former lives with people they had once loved, hated, and envied. Peter was shocked to realise that all around him at any given point was a wash of other consciousnesses, all weaving their way around the vastness of time. He met many, and at the same time met none.

Peter drifted from one place to another, until one day, who could say when, he met with the figure he had first seen all that time ago. "It's you" Peter said, "How long has it been my friend?" The figure smiled, without smiling, "Who can tell, Peter?"

Peter, although already knowing the answer, asked the figure one last question. "Who are you?" The figure looked deep into Peter, and a ray of the most brilliant warmth fell upon him. The figure spoke, but this time, with Peters voice. "You know who I am. I am Alfa and Omega. I am the beginning, and I am the end."

2.
The Corner of My Eye.

It was only there for a moment, but Steven could have sworn he saw a face at the window. He sat up, staring for a moment at the small single pane window next to the latch door. Telling himself he must have imagined it, he sank back into the large wing-backed armchair by the fire place, resuming his book and glass of port.

It had been a trying six months for Steven, with the divorce and financial settlements. All he had been left with was his small stone country cottage, nestled in the heart of the south downs, about a mile from Fulking, and a handful of shares that amounted to very little.

Still, as a writer he had the luxury of working from home, and given that he had never been a man of extravagance, he felt sure he could hang on just a few more months financially, and contact his publisher in the spring about his upcoming novel. After all, why should a divorce effect his popularity with his readers?

The radiant embers and dancing flames from the fire place bathed the room in a warm, orangey red glow, and the troubles of the day melted away as Steven took a long, luxurious pull on the vintage port.

Putting the book aside for a moment, he stood up and made his way over to the drinks cabinet, and proceeded to pour himself another drink. Pushing the cork back into the neck of the bottle with a satisfying squeak, he wondered to himself what his ex-wife was up to. Suddenly, there came a sharp tingle from the base of his spine that made its way up his back and hung like a cape over his shoulders. The face he thought he'd seen flashed back into his mind, and he turned his head over his left shoulder to look back at the small window. Nothing. Just small droplets of rain patting gently on the glass. Standing motionless for a second or two, his eyes made their way over to the latch door, with its knotted wood framing, and rusty metal hinges. The mood of the room changed. The once dancing red figures thrown out by the fire had turned into sharp tentacles, and his warm slipper clad feet had become cold and sweaty with anxiety. What had just happened?

Placing the glass on the side board, he slid gently over to the door, drawing back the top bolt, and grasping the latch. A childish surge bubbled up from the pit of his stomach, and the tips of his ears burned hot with anticipation. He unwillingly pushed the latch lock down with his thumb. The door pulled itself back into the room, revealing a dark, damp, windy world. The trees could just be made out in the gloom of the night as they thrashed back and forth in the wind, as if raging against some unknown evil hanging in the air.

Bracing one arm against the door frame, he lent his head out into the night air, turning his head quickly from left to right, hoping that he wouldn't see anything. Nothing. Just rain. What had come over him?

After shutting the door and returning the bolt, he sat himself back down by the fire, and jabbed at the embers with the steel poker. The cape of fear still hung over his shoulders, sinking deep into the base of his neck. The room fell into a bottomless dark rapture, and the dancing red tentacles leapt around the room, jumping out from the shadows as if trying to reach out for something to seize.

Steven shook his head, and tried to push the darkness from his mind. 'Don't be so silly', he said to himself as he got back up and made his way over to the side board to get his drink. Knocking the deep red liquid back in one, he shuddered as the strong fluid made its way into his system, tickling his throat as he swallowed. 'Time for bed'.

Ω

The following day put aside all thoughts of the night before, and Steven spent the morning chopping wood in the yard, and then in the afternoon he trudged over the downs on one of the many scenic walks that made up that part of the county. The weather wasn't great, and the grey clouds threatened rain. Only once did the clouds part to reveal a small pocket of blue sky that eventually disappeared into grey again. Heading back to the cottage, Steven's mind was occupied with thoughts of what he might do that evening. A spot of dinner, followed by a bit of light reading and an early night seemed like the way to go, and as he made his way down the winding tree covered track towards the cottage, he thought he could see someone waiting for him at the end of the path. He raised his hand in a gesture of greeting. As he did so, the figure appeared to acknowledge him, but rather than wave back, the figure simply turned and disappeared behind the grove of trees round the next bend.

A silence fell over the area. It felt as if Stevens ears had somehow been muffled. It was the kind of sensation one feels when swimming, and the water fills your ears to such an extent that for hours after you twist your jaw from left to right to try and relieve the pressure. He poked at his ears with his little figure, trying to release the numbness.

As the silence gently lifted, and the sound of his feet on the gravely path returned, he turned right at the end of the grove expecting to see the figure, but there was no one there. Thinking the person must have just been a walker on their way into Fulking he pushed the thought from his mind, and made his way over to the knotted front door of the cottage, turned the key in the lock and went indoors, closing the door behind him.

The fire which he had lit just before going out crackled softly at the end of the room, and Steven went through to the kitchen at the back of the cottage and started preparing the food for that evening's dinner.

$$\Omega$$

As the evening rolled around, Steven sat in the armchair by the fire feeling satisfied not only with the day he'd spent on the downs, but also with the food he had just finished. Wiping his mouth on his sleeve, he placed the empty plate on the small table by the armchair, and picked up his book. Not managing more than a few lines, the thought of the figure he'd seen that afternoon returned to him, and then the face he had or hadn't seen. Were the two things connected? Or was it all his imagination? Being alone can often put you in a strange frame of mind, and without anyone to talk to you can often allow your thoughts to run away with you. Just as Steven was contemplating this, the latch door shuddered against the frame. Steven, startled by the break in the silence, leapt up from the armchair. He stood, bent over slightly with one hand on his chest, and the other on his knee. It had taken him by surprise.

Had the door shuddered because of the wind, or had someone knocked? He pulled himself together, and cautiously opened the door. Nothing. In fact, it was pretty still. He closed the door and bolted it. Steven shook his shoulders, hoping it would dispel the dread that had been conjured in his mind. Sitting back in the chair, and looking over at the grandfather clock in the corner of the room, Steven wondered if it wouldn't better to just go to bed. It had been a long day, and it was obvious that his mind was playing tricks on him. He would give it another ten minutes, by which point it would be nine o'clock, then he would take himself up to bed.

Ω

As the clock chimed nine, Steven finished clearing up the last of the dishes in the kitchen, and turned off the lights, leaving the fire to burn itself out, and went to make his way up the small, tight staircase to his bedroom. But something stopped him just as he was about to ascend. Something at the back of his mind told him not to. It was odd. A cold, looming fear crept over him, and a strange sense that something upstairs that should be avoided made itself present. As he looked up the stairs to the landing, it was as if someone was staring back down at him. It was quite obvious that no one was there, but all his senses told him otherwise.

Steven, fixed in a state of unease, decided it would be best to sleep downstairs. He took the tartan blanket off the back of the armchair, sat himself down, and placed the thick cover over his lap. Despite his unease it wasn't long before he drifted off into a deep, and dreamless sleep, while the flickering red tentacles danced around the walls, branching off into the dark corners of the room.

Ω

It wasn't the grandfather clock chiming midnight that woke Steven up, or the periodic shudder of the door, but the sensation of dry leaves being gently stroked over his face, the sound of which was like someone slowly scrunching up a crisp packet. As he slowly opened his eyes, he could have sworn he saw someone in the room, standing in the corner by the kitchen door. It was enough to startle him, but only for a moment.

As sleep left him, and his waking senses returned, the figure was no more. Just a trick of the light. Steven dug the sleep from his eyes, and pulled the blanket up, and over his shoulders. The temperature of the room had dropped considerably. The fire had gone out.

Still a little groggy, Steven pulled himself up from where he had been sleeping. The firm leather of the armchair groaning as he did so, as if taking in a deep rasping breath of air. He clumsily made his way over to the kitchen to get himself a glass of water. His mouth was dry, almost feeling like it has been wrapped in tissue paper.

Getting a cup from the cabinet, and pouring himself a cool glass of water from the tap, he gulped it back in one. The smooth, clear liquid washed away the tissue paper, and he stood for a moment looking down into the large enamelled basin in front of him. The moonlight from the window in front of the sink illuminated the white enamel. The plug hole, stared up at him like a big black eye, never blinking, never removing its gaze.

Captured for a moment by the dark abyss beneath him, Steven's thoughts wondered. That was until, at the corner of his eye, he could see something out side of the window. His head jerked up. Outside, bathed in moonlight, on the left side of the path that lead into the drive of the cottage, a figure stood staring over towards the kitchen window. Steven rubbed his eyes. Another trick of the light? No, it was there. Frozen, and unable to blink, Steven just watched. And the figure, just watched back. Time stood still.

In that moment, all Steven could think to do, was to run into the living room, pick up the phone, and call someone. But Who? What would he tell them?
As the thought swirled in his mind, the figure began to move towards the house, lurching, sliding, rolling. Its movements were crooked and unnatural, almost as if every bone in its body was broken. It jerked and twisted, it flung, it writhed, it dragged. But all the while, Steven couldn't make out the details. The figure was black and shadowed, like a contorted black mass of distortion moving towards the house.
Steven's feet burned with cold stinging needles, traveling into his knees and creeping, sinisterly, up and over his shoulders, and into his chest. The fear was consuming.

It's at moments like this when that little child inside you takes control, and all logic is cast to the wind like a tree that drops it's leaves on a blustery Autumn day. Steven felt his heart thump in his chest, and the tendons in his hands tensed uncontrollably. Suddenly, there came the clink and crack of glass. Was it the window? No. A piercing pain in his right hand broke the tension. He looked down to find the glass in his hand was broken. The utter terror had unwillingly caused him to break the glass. Blood ran down his fingers, and dripped into the sink, mixing with droplets of water, and disappearing into the black eye at the centre of the enamelled basin.

A hot, uncontrollable rage boiled in Steven's body. An outrage, an anger unlike anything he had even felt before. His temples throbbed, and his eyes widened with animalistic fury. He flew from the kitchen, barging his way past the dining table chairs, which he sent flying across the room. He dragged his bloodied hand over the side board, knocking cups, candle sticks, and jugs onto the floor. Grabbing the poker from its rack by the fireplace, he went over to the front door, slung the bolt back, wrenched the door open, and ran out into the night.

'Come on then! Come on, lets have you!' Steven, brandishing the poker, jabbed and stabbed at the moon lit driveway, swinging left and right. He thrashed at the bushes, and tore at the trees. Cursing and spitting, he raged and whipped like a fish caught in a net. At one point, Steven insanely beat at the ground with the poker, throwing up gravel and dirt, and clumps of grass. His faculties misplaced, he swung the poker around his head, much like an Olympian would if they were to perform the hammer throw. Eventually, Steven over swung, and sent himself crashing down onto the gravel. He laid there, sprawled out over the driveway, staring up into the dark, inky blue sky above. His anger had evaporated. The gravel dug into the back of his head, and he could feel the pain in his cut hand return, throbbing intensely. But still he laid there, watching his breath disperse into the night. His lungs burned.

Ω

Who could say how long Steven laid there for? Eventually though, he pulled himself up, and dragged himself back over to the cottage, his hand sticky with drying blood, and his head aching from the release of tension.

As he entered the house, he simply slammed the door behind him, not even bothering to bolt it. Every fibre of his body was depleted of energy. Even making his way up the stairs proved difficult, as he lumbered up each step with increasing fatigue. He was even too tired to be afraid. The only thought running through his mind was bed, sleep, leaves… Bunches of leaves. Dropping the poker on the floor as he entered his bedroom, it hit the floorboards with a metallic clang that echoed across the room. He slumped onto the bed, lying motionless and drained. A cold sweat pearled and beaded on his forehead. Pulling his heavy arms up, he placed his hands on his stomach, feeling the sting of the cut as he did so. After a brief moment, his eyes slowly closed, and almost instantly Steven fell into a deep, dark, smothering sleep. While outside, the figure stood staring up at the bedroom window, waiting, watching.

Ω

It was hard to tell what time it was. It was still dark out, and the silence of the night hummed with a frequency that punctured the air. Sharp and slight.

Steven was still laying on the bed. His sleep was almost deathly. If it hadn't been for the slight movement in his chest, and the gentle rattle of his sleep rasp, you would be forgiven for thinking he was dead. His ashen, gaunt face betrayed no sense of life.

A swelling, suffocating air filled the room. An unseen pressure, thick and inky.

When Steven finally stirred from sleep, it was again to the sensation of dry leaves over his face. Opening his eyes, Steven rolled his vision around the room. Nothing but darkness. Steven could feel a weight against his chest, and he struggled to catch his breath against the hot stuffiness. Something was wrong. His position in the room had altered. It was as if he had shifted upwards towards the ceiling. His position, was all wrong.

There came a sharp grab at his ankles. An icy grip. The jolt caused his arms to drop from his stomach, and they hung down by his side, lifeless and numb. His head too dropped to the right, lolling dead in the air. What was happening?! His numb, unconscious body was being dragged through the aether, slowly, menacingly.

Steven's mind reeled in agony, but try as he might, he couldn't move. His body was dead, floating like a throttled fish on the water's surface, moving across the room, pulled by some unknown force, some unknown evil!

Trying to scream, and trying to fight, his mind bent, and cracked, and twisted with terror. The violence of his torment could be seen in his open eyes, which were wide and watery like glass, and red with pulsing fear. His mouth, aghast.

All turned to darkness…

Ω

A month later, on a crisp clear morning, two police squad cars were parked outside the small cottage. One of the officers was busying himself talking to one of the local farmers, and taking notes. Another, a tall police sergeant, was ducking his head under the low beams inside the cottage, and poking at the broken jugs on the sideboard with a pencil.

Upstairs, another two officers looked in puzzlement at the bedroom. Scattered all around the room, and on the bed, were piles and piles of dry leaves. The officers couldn't make head nor tail of it, and in the report they made that afternoon, they summarised that a window must have been left open at some point, and a storm blown them in.

If it hadn't been for Stevens ex-wife making the call to the Sussex police two days previous, and telling them that she hadn't heard from her ex-husband in weeks, the house may still have been left unmolested.

After a lengthy investigation, and multiple calls for the public to be on the lookout for a man fitting a fairly innocuous description, the police concluded that Steven had either skipped the country to avoid the legal payments of the divorce, or had potentially committed suicide.

Of course, we all know what happened on that dark night. We all know what it was at the window, and what it was standing at the end of the path. Don't we?

But if you're still a little unsure, I recommend you visit the Shepard and Dog pub in Fulking, and ask to speak to the landlord about Steven Bancroft. Sometimes he shakes his head, and says he's never heard of the man. But if he's in the right mood, and he takes a liking to you, he might tell you about that night, and the strange figure who walks the paths of rural Sussex… watching… waiting.

3.
Where are you?

As each footstep hit the sand, his legs got heavier and heavier. The sun beat down on his head with such ferocity, that it almost felt as if he was being scalped, and his bear arms tingled with an intense, burning red pain, as if being stuck with a million needles. But he had to go on! He simply had too!

With each passing day the great sand dunes loomed ever taller. Harder to climb, and even harder to see beyond. The sun boiled and flared, and the sand became as fine as dust. So fine in fact, that it got under his eyelids, making his eyes feel like marbles that someone had been playing with in the dirt. His feet were swollen and cracked, and his lips were puckered and crumbling. It was an endless, waking nightmare. He couldn't even remember the passing of the days. It was one long misery. An infinite trudge through an even more infinite desert.

Stopping, just for a moment, he dragged his creaking neck back to look up at the sky. The endless blue canopy above beat down on his mind, and the fragmenting spectrums of light danced and fizzed in his blurring vision. Purple, red, orange and yellow. Every particle of colour singed his thoughts. He fell to his knees.

Slumped, and unable to drag his head up from his chest, he slowly wheezed and rasped for air. His entire body was overcome by a vision of thousands of matches being scattered all over him. Each one hitting his withered body, and torturing every fibre of his leathery skin.
'I must go on!'

Ω

How long had he been wandering? How much further had he to go?
The hellishness played through his mind for what seemed like an eternity, until he eventually slumped forward, and his face hit the dusty sand with a low, dull flump.
Sprawled out on the sand, his eyes loosely shut, he drifted in and out of conciseness. The sun, still beating down on his pathetic body, clawing at the skin on the back of his neck.
Time drifted.

Ω

Darkness fell over the desert. In the moonlight, the great expanse of dunes turned into what looked like a white ruffled silk blanket. Calm, and gentle.

Still laying motionless on the dusty silk ocean, he opened his sand incrusted eyes. Forcing his eyes open, the lids stretched, glued together by a mixture of sweat, tears and sand, eventually parting and revealing a soup of blurred moonlight. The pain of doing so surged up through his temples and round to the back of his head.

As he gazed out across the desert, his perspective skewed by his horizontal state, the moon looked down on him with a cool, friendly smile.

With a sullen expression on his worn and cracked face, he basked in the coolness of the night. That was until a soft light patting on the sand came to his attention. His ears pricked up, as the low gentle patter got closer. With little or no strength left in him, he laid there helplessly. The only movement he could muster was to slowly close his eyes again, and hope it was just his imagination. But the pitter-patter was getting closer.

Even with his eyes closed, he could feel the presence of another, maybe two others, moving up alongside him. Pitter-patter, pitter-patter. As the presence neared he could hear the swish swish of material against material, the kind of sound denim trousers make when the inseam rubs against the other as you walk.

Dare he open his eyes?

He felt something light and soft touch his face. It patted at his cheek ever so gently, and then rested on his right temple. Whatever it was it was applying a small amount of pressure, and then rhythmically rubbing, softly, kindly. The scorching pain in his temples began to subside, and it was obvious that whoever, or whatever was before him, wasn't malign.
What was it?
He opened his eyes again. It was something dark and round. As his vision cleared, and the details came into focus, he couldn't quite believe his eyes. Was he really seeing this? Was he really seeing the black woollen face of a toy Golly Doll?

Ω

The Golly Doll stepped back, its small black woollen feet puffing gently into the sand. In its hand was a red lead, and attached to the lead was a small patchwork scotty dog with brown button eyes. The pair stood there, looking down at the wrinkled and worn figure laying in the sand.

After a brief moment, the Golly Doll turned its head and looked off into the distance, the blueness of the moon highlighting his beautiful round face, and adding life to his springy woollen curls.

The crinkled man in the sand just looked up at the pair, astounded. He wondered if he should say something. Or, perhaps he should just close his eyes again. But the compulsion to speak became overwhelming, and as he parted his lips to say something, the Golly Doll gently pulled at the lead, and the pair moved off across the dunes, with the tender sound of their feet puffing gently in the sand as they went.

Ω

Only a few minutes had past, but he felt compelled to follow the pair. He dragged his body up from the dust. Every inch of his mortal fibre creaked and groaned like an old wooden chair, and his skin felt as if it might tear like a dry leather bag. But he persisted.

Once on his feet he half heatedly brushed the dusty sand from his face, and followed the petite moonlit footprints left by the Golly and the dog. It was, he thought, a miracle that a breeze hadn't whipped up and blown the dainty little marks away.

Hugging his body, he carefully followed the path of prints over the dunes, looking up periodically at the moon. Hecate smiled back at him, and with every gaze up at her beautiful face he was bathed in the dark light of restitution.

Ω

It wasn't long before the dunes began to subside, giving way to a vast open expanse of flat land, surrounded by a crescent of seven mountains. And at its centre, a solitary body of water.
As he made his way down the bank of the last dune, he trod as carefully as possible, trying not to fumble. A couple of times he nearly over strode, but he managed to keep his composure, the clot of anticipation burning in his throat, the thirst for hydration.
When he finally made it to the base of the dunes he paused for a moment, looking in the direction of the small oasis at the centre of the vast blue expanse, just checking it wasn't a trick of the mind, or a mirage. Half-naked, and half destroyed he staggered across the soft rockless earth, its cool embrace hugging the sides of his feet like a mattress hugs a prostrate sleeping body.
About ten yards from the glistening pool, he noticed the Golly and his little quilted companion sitting by the bank, still and quiet. They paid him no attention as he bumbled passed them and threw himself headlong into the deep cooling embrace of the inky blue body of water. As he slipped beneath the surface, the rapture of its hold coursed through his frail body, and he took in great gulps of the clear sweet water. He could have drowned then and there, but he wouldn't have cared. Not one iota.

Ω

When he finally emerged from the water, he burst through the reflection of the moon, which sent sparkling ripples of shimmering glass across the pool. The swelling waves emanated out from the now reborn figure at their centre. The Golly stood up and watched, as the man wadded with great vigour and renewed vitality back to the shore. His face clean and smooth, his body like steel, his eyes like thunder. The mountains smiled.

Throwing himself down by the bank, he rested his forearms on his knees and breathed deeply, the clear night air ecstatically stinging his lungs. Peace.

Whilst lost in thought, the man didn't notice the Golly approach him. He startled ever so slightly at the gentle, woolly pat on his shoulder.

Turning to look, the Golly gestured in the direction of a small bush on the other side of the pool. There, bathed in brilliance, something could be seen emerging from behind its thorny branches. What was it?

Oh, this was too much! A toy cow.

The man didn't bother to rub his eyes in disbelief. He simply sat there and watched. After the cow, other figures began to emerge. A horse, made from wood. A cat, with a bell attached to the end of its tail. A pheasant, wearing a sugar-loaf hat. And to top it all off, a flying kipper, swirling through the night air as if dancing, with its butterflied fillets flapping against the stillness.

And there he was, a man. A simple, half naked man sitting in the sand.

Ω

It was obvious to the man that this was some sort of occasion, and that the assembled band of characters had come with some purpose in mind. What it was though, he couldn't be sure. Standing up, and placing his hands on his hips, he watched. The small group on the other side of the bank were busying themselves with something, but he couldn't quite see what. Collecting something perhaps? As he wondered to himself, he felt a light tap on his thigh. It was the Golly and his dog. He looked down at them, and the Golly smiled back.

The gentle little doll took the man's hand, and again pointed in the direction of the group on the other side of the bank. They were still busying themselves with some task or other, and as the man and Golly made their way around the bank of the pool towards them, he noticed that it was dry knotted pieces of wood that they were collecting.

Upon reaching the little band, the Golly and his dog padded their way over to the group, and sat by the small pile of twigs and branches that had been collected. The Golly reached into his red jacket pocket and produced a box of matches, and set about lighting a fire.

Suddenly, the rough pile of twigs burst into flames, sending a large woosh of orange into the air, which after a moment or two finally settled back down among the crackling fingers of wood. All of the assembled gathered around the fire and basked in the glory of its light and warmth, each one staring deep into the flames, as if waiting for an apparition. All except the flying kipper, which happily, and silently, swooped above them.

Ω

As the time passed, the man's gaze shifted from the strange collection of characters around him, to the shimmering, dancing lights of the fire. His eyes locked on the twirling, whipping jolts of flame. As he sat watching, something stirred in the deep red embers, something taught, something deep, something real…

As if compelled by some unseen force, all sat around the fire looked up, their heads thrown back by a cooling blast of what the man could only think of as divine energy. Beams of brilliant white light coursed from the fire and shot into the star dotted sky above. The man could feel something happening to his body, something beyond anything he had ever felt before!

His entire being was filled with life, but not anything that could be explained as earthly, or physical, but what he could only explain as a celestial separation of his very fibre. He was at once both terrified and rapturous. Moving his eyes to the right, not wanting to move his body for fear that this great experience might suddenly end, he witnessed the Golly Doll and his dog being consumed by an internal light that emanated from there very being, and in that moment, they fragmented into small particles of shining dust, that in turn dispersed into the ether.

He moved his gaze back to the fire, and within the brilliant flames emerged two golden winged cherubim, their heads bowed in supplication, and their wings pointed forward meeting at their tips. It was then that he understood, as his vision slowly became enveloped by brilliance, as his own internal light began to consume him. The journey through the desert, how he got there, where he was from, his beginnings. All these things suddenly made perfect sense, and at the same time became meaningless, as the joyous rays of radiant light and energy burst through the gaps between atoms that made up his physical being.

The last thing he saw as he gazed up into the heavens, witnessing this great conversion, was the flying kipper, which flew up and up into the warm embrace of the light.

4.
Flowers and Flags.

Johann reached up for the next ledge. He grasped at the rock, bringing his foot up and digging his crampon clad boot into the side of the mountain.

'One last heave', he thought, as he pulled himself up the craggy incline just a few more inches. 'One more meter to go!'

Carefully making sure that his right foot was well placed, Johann swung the other over and up to the left, and dug it into a small break in the rock, and using this, he then levered himself up another foot.

It was the perfect weather for climbing. It was clear, it was sunny, and it was still.

Below him was the rest of the team, all following the line and signalling to the next where to place their feet, and where they could find the best grip on the rock.

There is something very special about climbing. Often people imagine it's the thrill of danger that possesses one to go scaling a mountain. But, to the true climber it's about skill and determination. Peace and tranquillity. The reward for all the hard work comes when you finally reach the summit, and take in the scale and majesty of it all.

Johann pulled himself up another foot or two, and then reached up with his left hand to get a purchase on the rock. With his right hand he griped his pick axe, and swung it over the ledge above him. It sunk with a satisfying crack into the stony earth.

He pushed up. His legs burned with the strain of hauling not only himself, but the bergen on his back too, which weighed half as much as himself. But finally, he made it! Three days of hard climbing were over.

The last scramble over the edge, and it was done. Johann got to his feet, and immediately set about hammering a piton into the ground, and tying off the rope into a bowline knot. He gave it a sharp tug to signal to the others that they could continue to climb, and then took his bergen off and set in on the ground, taking a moment to gaze off into the distance, and catch his breath.

$$\Omega$$

After the others had finally made it up too, they all went about their individual tasks. Johann instructed two of them to set up the cooker and prepare some food and boil some water for coffee. He then got the other three to do a light survey of the summit, and access its viability for a climber's cabin in the future.

As for himself, Johann got out his small note book, and made a few calculations on the time it took to ascend, and some of the finer points of their equipment. What was necessary, and what could be left behind int the future.

After this, he then went and checked on the two members of the team who were preparing lunch. 'All in hand?' he asked. The other two looked up and nodded, handing him an enamelled mug of steaming hot coffee. 'Thanks'.

Johann took his coffee and bergen over to a more secluded area and sat himself down on a rock. Looking out over the landscape he thought to himself how beautiful it all was. In the distance, on the other side of the valley, capped by hats of snow were other more impressive mountains, the sun's rays bouncing off the snow at their peak, making them shimmer like glass.

As he followed the outline of these goliaths down into the valley, he noticed the small alpine shepherd huts, and the light dotting of rural chalets, all of which he imagined had skis propped up outside against the wood sheds, or beautiful alpine flowers grown in pots on the window siles, tended to by kindly faced old ladies.

From his perch, he also noticed what looked to be a herd of cattle being driven through the valley from the right and past one of the houses. It was hard to make them all out, but they were defiantly cattle, as he could hear the distant clang of the bells around their necks. It was incredible, he thought, that the sound was able to travel so far.

He took a sip of his coffee. As he did, he noted a small cluster of rocks by his feet, and growing from this cluster, five Edelweiss. He lent down and gently picked one. Admiring its delicate colour and robust features, he then poked the end of the stem into the lapel of his woollen tunic. It was rare to find Edelweiss, even at these hights. They needed very specific conditions, and even if the conditions were correct, it didn't automatically mean you would find them. He quietly whispered to himself. 'luck? No, destiny'.

Ω

By the time everyone had finished their jobs and eaten, the sun had shifted across the sky and caught the ripples of the stream down in the valley. The twinkles of light danced around the water like fireflies.

Johann was reminded of his childhood, as he looked back down at the alpine chalets and pastures bellow. Long summers spent outdoors with friends, crisp winters out on the slopes skiing with his father, and weekly trips into town with his mother. If he was lucky, she'd buy him something sweet from the bakery.

That was twenty years ago now. But it was reassuring to think that even though his mother and father had passed on, and the local town had become busier over time, this place here, this wonderful spot up in the mountains remained constant, with the promise of a better future, ever present on the mountain clad horizon.

Johann was brought back to the present by a light breeze. It sprung up out of nowhere, and calmly broke against his wind smock. The air carried with it a sweet, clean, unmolested freshness that remined Johann of cut grass. It only lasted a few seconds, and then as quickly as it came, it was gone again. Disappearing into the atmosphere once more.

What joy. What beauty. What wonder!

Ω

Johann brought his binoculars up, and perched his hat back on his head a little. Looking out over the valley, he made a mental note of the best way to climb the mountain opposite. How long would it take? Hard to say. Anyway, it wasn't of any immediate concern, they would get themselves back down into the valley, set up camp, and then beguine the decent proper the following day. Hopefully the weather would hold out. Even if it didn't it wouldn't matter, it just meant they would have to spend a little longer up there, and for seasoned mountain climbers this was no issue at all. The fact of the matter was, they loved it.

Johann pulled himself together, and packed the last few bits of equipment into his bergen, pulling the cord closure tight and buckling the flap down firmly. The only things he left out were two flags on telescopic polls, which he proceeded to open out.

He unravelled one, which displayed their team's military division, with the relevant Edelweiss flower carefully embroidered underneath. It read, *2. Gebirgs-Division.*

He stuck this into the ground, and gave the end of the poll three hard wakes with his hammer. He then took the other flag, and repeated the process.

Ω

After they had all packed up, gearing themselves up for the decent, they all took one last look at their beautiful surroundings.

Johann took it all in. The mountains and the valley, the stream flanked by quaint alpine houses, the distant clang of bells, and of course their national flag flapping gently in the wind. And at its centre, a bold black swastika.

5.
The Tealeaf.

It didn't belong to her, but she didn't care, she wanted it! Need didn't even play a part in her decision. She took the small wooden box off the shelf and eyed the exquisite workmanship. Beautiful scrolling, with antler and brass inlay, and the finest carved rosses around its circumference. It must have taken the craftsman a considerable amount of time to make, and it showed.

Looking carefully from right to left, she made sure no one was looking and gently slipped the box into her bag. It rested deep and heavy at the bottom. Would anyone notice when she left the shop?

Casually, she sauntered through the shop to the exit, feigning interest in other items as she went. She slipped by the lady behind the desk, smiled, and waltzed out the shop and down the road.

It was a buzz, a thrill, a swindle. And she loved every moment of it!

Ω

As she drove home, the bag with the box in it resting on the front passenger seat next to her, she shifted gears with a cocky air of accomplishment. It was the feeling of getting one over on people that she really got off on. 'Sticking to the man' she would often say to herself. She had some crack pot ethical argument for stealing, and that there are the 'haves' and 'have nots' in society, but at the end of the day, deep down, she knew it was a load of bollocks.
She stopped at the traffic lights and shifted the gears into first, her foot depressed on the break. In front was a small fiat 500 in yellow. She kept her gaze on the lights, waiting for them to change, whilst she impatiently rapped her acrylic nails on the steering wheel.
Amber, green. "Come on, for fuck sake!" she screamed as the car in front failed to get going. "What are you, blind, you dick head!?" She thumped at the horn.
Eventually the small yellow fiat got going, turning left and allowing her the pull away fast and impatiently up the main road. "Stupid old bag", she said under her breath, as she pushed the car into second and drove the last ten minutes back home.

Ω

Unloading her shopping from the car, she slammed the boot with a gratifying low thump. It was the sound of quality that you often get with expensive cars when you close their doors. And posh it was too, A BMW 4 series coupe, it was metallic blue and had cost her just shy of £36,000. As it was, parked on the driveway of her semi-detached four-bedroom home, she always thought it looked good, sitting powerfully for all the neighbours to see. Walking up to the porch she opened the front door, and went straight through the hallway to the kitchen, putting the bags down on the marble worktop. One by one she went through the bags and decanted the weekly shop into the cupboards, fridge, and freezer.

If it hadn't had been for a light knock behind her as she was putting the cornflakes onto the top shelf, she might not have turned round. For as she did, the box, which she'd pinched not an hour ago, was sitting front and centre on the kitchen counter.

"I didn't unpack you, did I?" she said to herself as she walked over to it. Looking down on the box again, she felt the light spurt of excitement pulse through her chest. The box was beautiful, extremely beautiful. In fact, the natural light from the window enhanced its beauty all the more. The deep hand tooled work, complimented by the polishing and inlay took on a life of its own. The knots and curls of the wood, like paths and streams on a map.
Her eyes twinkled with joy.

Ω

Pouring herself a glass of white wine, she took the box into the softly furnished cream and stone coloured living room, sitting herself luxuriantly into the sofa.
With the box on her lap, she sipped some wine. "Oh, you are clever, aren't you Lucy", she commented to herself, looking down at her little accomplishment for the day, "Oh so very clever".
The brass inlay caught the light divinely, and as she rocked the box up and down on her lap with her thighs, the golden reflection shot back and forth across the lid. And then, it came again, the light knocking. Dumbfounded, Lucy looked around the room. Nothing. And then again, knock, knock, knock. Whatever it was, it was coming from inside the box.

Ω

Putting the wine down on the glass coffee table, Lucy sat up and looked down on the small wooden container. It had grown heavy, far heavier than when she had stolen it. The weight was unbearable, and the corners of the box dug into her legs. What was causing this? She tried to lift it up and off her lap, but it was too heavy. It just sat there, pushing down into her muscles. Tears began to roll uncontrollably down her face as she struggled to remove it, wrenching it back and forth with all her might, but it wouldn't budge. Her feet started turning blue from the pressure, and the veins on her legs bulged as she felt every pulsing thump of her heart in the back of her knees trying to pump the blood around the body. The pain was excruciating!

As if from nowhere, a voice in her head said "open, open." Could she? Could she open the box, or would the lid prove just as heavy? All that ran through Lucy's mind was the thought that the box, getting heavier and heavier, would cut through her legs completely, leaving her screaming in hopeless agony, and unable to walk ever again.

Flashing her hand forward, she braced it against the corner of the lid, and flipped it open. A vast, thrashing woosh of air burst out from the container, and shot out into the room. The pressure on her legs was relieved, and she slumped back into the sofa, kicking the box from her lap onto the floor.

The relief was sweet, but she barely had time to enjoy it, as the monumental blast of air whipped up and twirled through the living room like a tornado, sending anything it came into contact with hurtling through the air. At one point it picked up the television and sent it across the other side of the room, smashing it into the wall with such force that it exploded into thousands of shards of black plastic. Some of these pieces hit Lucy in the side of the face and arm causing deep cuts and gashes, but this was the least of her problems.

$$\Omega$$

After thirty seconds or so, the whirl of air and furniture finally settled down, throwing what was left of Lucy's belongings onto the cream pile carpet in broken and torn pieces. But it wasn't over, because in its place was a terrifying beast. It loomed down on her, its dreadful eyes focused directly into hers, and its mouth open and waiting, jagged and sharp.

There wasn't even time to scream. The beast reached out with its talon like hand and grabbed Lucy by the waist. Holding her aloft for a few seconds, she just had time to gaze at the creatures back tilted head, and through the pain in her body she realised, it was over.

The beast thrust her like a rag doll into its mouth, slamming its muscular jaw down on her repeatedly, over and over again. In less than five seconds it was over. Crunched, chewed, pulped, and swallowed.
Lucy the tealeaf was no more. But out on the driveway was her BMW 4 series coupe sitting powerfully, for all the neighbours to see.

The End.

Printed in Poland
by Amazon Fulfillment
Poland Sp. z o.o., Wrocław